W9-BYF-881

Indescribably Arabella

written and illustrated by Jane Gilbert

An Anne Schwartz Book
Atheneum Books for Young Readers
New York London Toronto Sydney Singapore

For my darling daughters, Reny and Taly,
because they grew up with Arabella

Atheneum Books for Young Readers
An imprint of Simon & Schuster Children's Publishing Division
1230 Avenue of the Americas, New York, New York 10020

Book design by Jane Gilbert and Ann Bobco
The text for this book is hand lettered by Tad Hills in the style of Jane Gilbert.
The illustrations for this book are rendered in gouache.
Manufactured in China
First Edition
10 9 8 7 6 5 4 3 2 1
Library of Congress Cataloging-in-Publication Data
Gilbert, Jane.
Indescribably Arabella / Jane Gilbert.— 1st ed.
p. cm.
"An Anne Schwartz Book."
Summary: An unusual young girl, upon deciding to become famous, tries painting, acting, and dancing, but is disappointed in the results until a lonely old couple encourages her to do things her own way.
ISBN 0-689-85321-1
[1. Individuality—Fiction. 2. Fame—Fiction.] I. Title.
PZ7.G3744 In 2003
[Fic]—dc21
2002001938

Arabella Anastasia
was not
an ordinary girl.
She was, well,
indescribably Arabella.
One day Arabella
decided to be famous.
She pondered
on how to do it and...

ALL OF A SUDDEN SHE KNEW!

I shall become a famous painter.

So she painted

and

painted

and

painted.

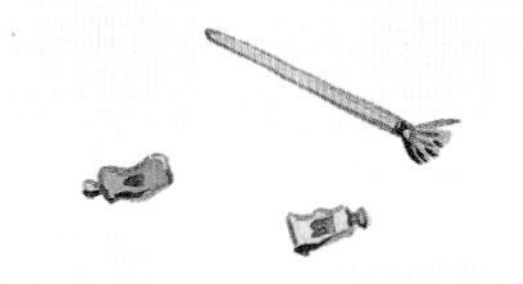

And she tried to
make her paintings
as beautiful as all
the other paintings
she had seen.
But her colors
always ran together
and the lines
were always
CROOKED.

"I am sorry," her art teacher said, "but you will never be a famous painter."

So Arabella
went home
and put
her paintings
away.

And she pondered and pondered
on how to become famous.

ALL OF A SUDDEN SHE KNEW!

I shall become a famous actress.

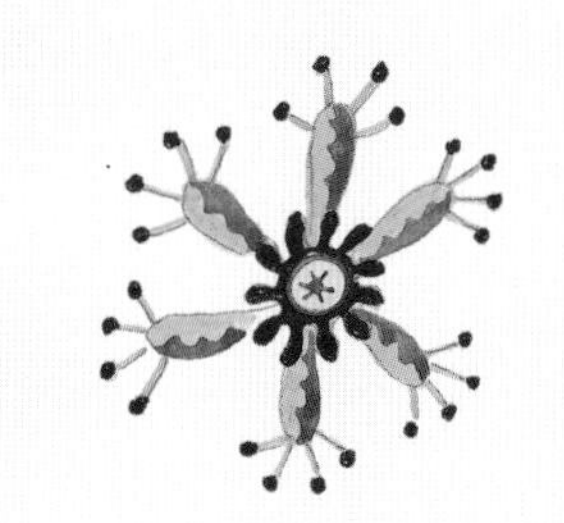

Arabella Anastasia

was not an ordinary person,
you must remember. She was, well,
indescribably Arabella. And she did want
to become famous so badly!

So she acted

and

acted

and

acted.

And she tried to act like all the other famous actors she had seen. But her entrances were always late

and she could never remember her lines.

"I am sorry," her
acting teacher said,
"but you will never
be a famous actress."

Arabella tried not to be downhearted.

With her last few pennies she bought a ballet dress and dancing slippers.

"I will teach myself to dance," she said.
And she practiced and...

practiced and practiced and practiced . . .

...till she could

leap

and

whirl

and

kick

and

stand on her toes like all the other famous dancers she had seen.

But no one would even look at Arabella dance. The people in the Big Offices just laughed at her short legs and her funny little voice because she was, well, indescribably Arabella, and they turned her away from their doors.

"Oh, dear!" cried Arabella. "I shall never become famous!"
And she went out to the trash and threw out her paints, and her costumes, and her dancing slippers.

Two little old people who were very lonely and very sad were passing by, and they said to her, "Why are you doing that, my dear?"

"No one appreciates me," Arabella said,
and she sat down and told her whole story.

The two little old people, who
were very lonely and very sad,
took Arabella Anastasia,
her paints, her costumes,
and her dancing slippers
home with them.

"Now please paint a picture for us, Arabella."

So Arabella Anastasia painted her own kind of picture. It was of their cat, and it was the most unusual picture that the two little old people had ever seen. They hung it right up over their fireplace.

"Now act out a little play
for us, Arabella."
So Arabella Anastasia
acted in her own kind
of way, and it was the
most unusual performance
that the two little old
people had ever seen.
They clapped and clapped.

"Now please dance, Arabella, for you make us very happy."

So Arabella

K
I
C
K
E
D

and TURNED...

. . . and

J
U
M
P
E
D

and

W
H
I
R
L
E
D . . .

. . . all in her own special way. And the two little old people were so very happy and LOVED Arabella's dancing so very much that they clapped and clapped their hands. Now Arabella performs for the whole neighborhood, so you see she HAS become famous after all.

And she is also, always, indescribably Arabella.

HAWN MEMORIAL LIBRARY
0 11 06 0004465 2